Vampire
Dawn

In Cold Blood

ANNE ROONEY

Ransom

Hungary, August ...

Juliette, Omar, Finn, Ruby and Alistair find a dead body in the forest ...

... Twenty-four hours later, they tie the murderer, Ava, to a tree, as one by one they fall sick ...

... When they wake, they are vampires, and that murderer looks rather appealing ...

... Mysterious nobleman Ignace, 400 years old and more sophisticated than is good for him, prevents them snacking on her ...

... But that dead body isn't as dead as it looked ...

... They go to Ignace's castle for a crash-course in being a modern vampire.

And so their adventures begin.

This is Ava's story ...

One

Ava hit the ground and rolled, the freezing snow bringing her quickly to her senses. Tyres squealed.

It took her a moment to sit up, brush the snow from her face and look around. The car that had dumped her was gone. No one looked at her. She struggled to her feet, feeling dazed and bruised, and knocked more snow from her coat. It was a fur coat – not hers. She looked down. Her feet were snug in Ugg boots, and they weren't hers either. Thoughts swam into her head:

Where am I? How did I get here?

One hand clenched something tightly. She opened her fist and looked at a hotel key – a real key with a heavy fob engraved 'Hotel Star Pristina'.

What's this? What's going on?

She could see the hotel the other side of the road. She stumbled, hurt and confused, over the road to the hotel entrance and showed the key to a doorman, who said something she didn't understand.

At reception, a woman with bleached hair and thick glasses looked up and said something that again Ava didn't understand.

Ava showed her the key.

'Ah, we've been expecting you,' the woman said in English. 'Your room is ready. Your – er, friend – has paid in advance. You've been unwell, I hear. Do you have luggage?'

Ava shook her head, and it hurt. Where were her things? All the stuff she had brought to Europe? She had no idea. The woman looked her up and down – disapproving, Ava thought – then led her upstairs to her room.

'Here.' The woman opened the door, then stalked off.

The room was large and comfortable – and there were her clothes, neatly folded on the bed, along with some new, warm things that suited the weather.

Where am I? she thought.

Ava pulled the heavy velvet curtains shut against the snow and flopped onto the bed, suddenly tired. Within seconds she was asleep – a long, dreamless sleep that lasted until the next afternoon.

* * * * *

When Ava woke, she felt groggy and empty. When had she last eaten? She didn't know.

An image flashed into her mind. A tray of food, a room in an old castle. She hadn't wanted the food, even though it was really good food. Was it Ignace's castle in Hungary? She didn't think so.

She wasn't really hungry, just empty. It was a strange feeling, but quite pleasant. She thought eating would make her sick.

She found a street map on the desk – Pristina,

Kosovo.

That must be where I am, she thought. *In Kosovo! But how? Why?*

She suspected Ignace had something to do with it. That fleeting image – she tried to bring it back – was he anywhere in it? She thought she saw ... someone. Omar – was that possible?

Ava wrapped herself in the fur coat and headed out into the street. She trudged through snow and slush, past people who kept their heads down.

At dusk she came to a bleak park. The snow was grey here, and churned into rucks and ridges. A group of trailers huddled in a clearing between the trees. They were dejected, with peeling paint and cracked wood. No one was around – it was far too cold to be out – but smoke curled from blackened tin flues.

Crude pictures on the trailers showed trapeze artists, clowns, a tiger.

It's a circus, Ava thought. *But pitched in Kosovo in the winter – it must be the worst circus in the world!*

She would have steered clear a few months ago, afraid of the tough, gypsy types and their fierce dogs. Now she talked herself out of being scared.

'I've been attacked by vampires, dragged to a vampire castle, left alone in Prague, then – then something I don't even remember,' she said aloud to herself. 'What's the point in worrying? If something happens, I'll cope.'

She walked between the dingy trailers. Something strange and compelling pulled her forwards, despite her fear. She followed the feeling, and it caught in her throat. Excitement. *Why? I don't even like circuses*, she thought. But it was something more basic, in her gut. Hunger. But unlike any hunger she'd felt before.

Ava stopped where the feeling was strongest, beside a shabby trailer. She walked all around. It had a flat base and then bars all the way to the roof. She should leave. But she couldn't go. She peered into the gloom.

There in the corner was a curled shape, with a slowly moving head. As Ava's eyes adjusted to the gathering dark she saw a tail thumping heavily on the wooden floor. The stripes of light and shadow were not just cast by the bars of the cage, but were part of the shape.

The tiger moved a heavy paw to hold down a hunk of meat as it chewed. Its amber eyes looked straight at her. Ava wanted the meat – no, she *needed* the meat. She had no idea why. There were two pieces: one under the tiger's paw and a smaller piece near the bars. She could reach it if she dared. She could reach it, and daring didn't come into it.

She waited until the tiger's head was down, chewing, and then pushed a hand through the bars towards the smaller piece. The sleeve of the fur coat didn't fit, it got stuck. But now the tiger was looking at her. She didn't care. She struggled out of the coat and dropped it, then slipped her arm easily between the bars.

The tiger snarled.

'Shhhhh,' she said. 'There, there. Nice tiger.'

One paw stretched out, lazy at first, then lightning fast. It swiped her arm and slashed it from elbow to wrist. Ava screamed, pulled back her ravaged arm and stared in horror at the gaping wound, waiting for the blood to flow.

And she waited.

The sides of the parted muscle stood pink and firm, but unbloodied. She screamed again. And again and again. Very slowly, a trickle of red formed inside the cut. It was like a river in a valley, fed by streams, but all in slow motion.

Ava watched in horror, too afraid to feel the pain. And too afraid to notice the person approaching from behind, until a hand covered her mouth and an arm clamped across her chest.

Two

Ava bit the hand that was over her mouth. Another hand came up, replacing it. The arm was bare – astonishing in the cold – and it was a woman's arm, but thick and strong.

'Let me go!' Ava tried to shout, but her voice was muffled by the arm.

Ava bit again, as hard as she could, and suddenly felt warm blood in her mouth. She kept her teeth in the flesh, then dug them in harder, and sucked without thinking and without feeling anything but a flood of pleasure.

The woman swore and hit Ava around the head, hard, so that she fell over. Then the woman stood nursing her arm and looking at Ava, with blood around her mouth, lying in the snow.

Ava's arm, ripped open, was barely bleeding. The woman stared at it and started to back away. Ava licked the blood from her lips and lunged towards the woman's ankle, mouth gaping, desperate for more.

The woman turned and ran, shouting: 'Lugat, lugat!'

Ava had no idea what it meant. No one came from any of the trailers or caravans. Indeed, lights went out – no one was going to help the woman.

Left alone, Ava grabbed a handful of blood-spattered snow and filled her mouth with it, desperate for every last drop of the blood, faint with the longing for more. But the woman was gone, and Ava didn't dare try again to take meat from the tiger.

A distant scream, that could have been a person or an owl, roused Ava. She looked around. Was that a dark figure, hurrying through the trees? She wasn't sure. Perhaps it was just a shadow. She picked up her coat and made her way slowly back to the city.

She found a restaurant with a menu in English. When the waiter came back, she pointed to 'steak'. He asked her a question which she didn't understand. She took the pen from him and drew on his pad – a steak dripping with blood. He laughed.

Ten minutes later he brought her a steak that

was barely cooked – a large slab of bleeding meat. Ava was so excited she struggled to eat it with a knife and fork. She longed to pick it up in her hands and bite, sucking the blood from it like you would suck juice from an orange.

* * * * *

Back at her hotel, the meaning of it all struck her. The meaning and the horror. What had she become? She hardly dared think about it.

Ava made excuses in her head. She was confused, she had lost her memory, she hadn't eaten for ages.

It was impossible that she was a vampire – that was ages ago, in summer. The others became vampires overnight. Of course it couldn't have happened to her. Everything would be fine tomorrow. Perhaps she was just anaemic, needed iron in her diet. That must be it.

But she couldn't fool herself. She woke in the silent, early hours of the morning, startled by dreams of blood that made her desperate with longing.

In Hungary, Ignace had made her eat bread soaked in Nathan's blood. He'd said it would make her immune. Nathan. Her ex-boyfriend who'd tried to kill her. Well, bite her. She shuddered.

He must have felt the same about her as she'd felt about the woman at the circus. She'd wanted to suck the woman's blood, more than she'd ever wanted anything. It was a terrifying need. She knew she couldn't control it.

Ava struggled to fill the gaps in her memory. Maybe there was a clue in the time she'd forgotten.

Remember, she told herself. *You must remember what happened.*

After Ignace's castle she'd gone to Prague. She'd been walking, and someone had called her name. And then nothing – except that flashback to a room in a castle and a meal she didn't want. And perhaps Omar. But that didn't make sense. The next thing she knew, she was here, chucked out of a moving car, with a hotel key and a fur coat that wasn't hers.

Ava went into the bathroom and looked at her reflection in the mirror. She had a reflection. *Surely vampires had no reflection?* she thought. Perhaps the reflection faded slowly.

Suddenly, fury overwhelmed her. She grabbed the marble soap dish and hurled it at the mirror, smashing her image into dozens of tiny reflections. If she had to be a vampire, she was going to be an angry one. She picked up a piece of the shattered mirror and ran her finger along the sharp edge.

Three

Ava couldn't read the poster in the hotel lobby, but one word leapt out at her: '*Vampir*'. The circus had a vampire called Ivan. There was a picture of him – a boy of about her own age, fit, wearing a black cloak and with pointy teeth exposed and dripping blood. She asked the stern woman at reception, who shrugged.

'He says he's a vampire. What do I know? It's a circus – they have all types. Go and see if you like it. It is open tonight.'

Six months ago, she'd have assumed he was a fake. Now she knew he might not be. She had to find out. She'd go to see it. And then, if he was a real vampire ... Was it too much to hope for?

The park was swarming with police, and they'd cordoned off the area near the trailers. Ava skirted around it to the queue of families waiting to see the circus. As they filed into the striped Big Top and hustled for the best seats, she curled her fingers around the razor-sharp shard of mirror she'd put in her pocket. If she could just get close enough, she'd see if he had a reflection.

It was a cold night to sit in a tent. Ava could see the tiger's breath as it prowled sulkily and did easy tricks. Ava pushed her left hand inside the right sleeve of her coat and felt the makeshift bandage she'd put on her arm. She should have had the wound stitched – it would scar horribly. And it ached. She felt sure the tiger was looking at her, knowing. For how many centuries would she carry that scar? Ava wondered.

The vampire boy came on stage dressed in a cape. He had dark hair, slicked back, and pointy teeth – a standard, movie vampire. He acted out a dinner scene with a girl in a skimpy dress, eating a raw steak while the girl looked nervous.

The vampire drank red liquid from a glass, and the girl refused to drink. Then he tried to bite the girl, but she fought him off with a crucifix. He recoiled, and then bit a hapless dog and sucked some of its blood. He *had* bitten it – or it was a good fake – and he had blood dribbling down his chin.

Ava wasn't sure she believed the act. She knew

she wouldn't waste any blood like that. But he'd had practice. And perhaps he would finish the dog later.

She left at the interval, hoping to catch the vampire boy outside. He was leaning against a trailer, drinking from a brown bottle. Blood? Beer? She went over.

'Hi. Do you speak any English?' she asked.

'Yep. Lots. And you?'

Ava was stunned.

'You're English?' she said.

'I am. You're not.'

'Australian,' she said.

'What are you doing in a dump like this in the middle of winter?'

Ava shrugged. She actually didn't know.

'I just ended up here.' She didn't think she could say – 'I went off with some vampires and then something happened that I don't remember and I found myself here.'

'Want a drink?' He waved the bottle at her.

'What is it?'

'Blood.'

She took it – perhaps too eagerly – and knocked it back. It wasn't blood.

'I'm impressed,' he said. 'Most girls would have refused.'

'It's not very nice,' she said. 'What is it really?'

'Some local brew. We could go for a normal

drink if you like?'

She did like, and they went to a small café. She felt
drawn to Ivan. There was something about him that
entranced her. Perhaps it was the vampire in him. Or
perhaps it was his perfectly chiselled features, his easy
manner, his ready smile and the way he touched her arm.

'So, tell me about your act. Are you a real
vampire?' she asked.

'Can't tell you. Trade secret.'

How could she tell him it was her trade, too?
No, not on a first date. She'd tell him soon.

They talked and talked, and when they both
ordered rare steak, he laughed.

'Really? You really want it?' he asked. But when
it came, it was very clear that she really wanted it.

four

The next day, Ava woke feeling weak and shaky. Was she ill? Or just – she didn't like to think of it – hungry? She remembered Ivan and a warm glow crept around the edges of her hunger. He'd given her his number, but when she called it went straight to voicemail.

'This is Ivan the vampire. I'm sleeping in my coffin just now. Please leave a message.'

Then there was a bit more in a foreign language.

'Ivan – it's Ava. I wondered if you'd like to meet up today. Maybe? Call me? If you like. Not if you don't want to. Obviously. Er. Bye.'

She felt stupid. She called again.

'When you get out of your coffin, you lazy vampire, meet me for a blood-fest, yes?'

By late evening he hadn't called. She was faint with need, so went back to the café alone, but it was closed.

She could smell the blood in everyone who passed her in the street. It made her think of following them, sinking her teeth into their flesh. She was horrified by these fantasies, but couldn't get them out of her mind. She looked around her hurriedly. A tall man in a long, dark coat was watching her from a distance. When she saw him, he quickly turned away. Ava stared at his back. She didn't like him looking at her, it made her anxious.

She pulled the fur coat tight against the swirling snow and turned a corner into an empty street. A girl stood near a taxi sign, shivering in a cheap coat. Her high heels slipped in the snow. She looked as if she'd been to a party.

The girl blew on her fingers and pulled them inside her coat sleeves. She was about Ava's age. She glanced at Ava and smiled, but guilt strangled any wish Ava had to smile back. She walked past the girl, shaking with nerves but knowing what she would do, unable to stop herself.

Ava leaned against a wall and pretended to send

a text while she looked around. She couldn't see the man in the coat. She lunged forwards, grabbed the girl's neck, and dragged her between two buildings.

The girl struggled, but Ava pulled the long sliver of mirror from her pocket and brought it to the girl's throat.

Huge, frightened eyes stared above Ava's hand clamped over the girl's mouth. *No, not the neck*, Ava thought. *She mustn't die.* She grabbed a wrist and slashed it once, then pulled it up to her mouth, ignoring the screams that started as soon as Ava moved her hand away from the girl's mouth.

She sucked, and her head swam with delight. It was like a drug – she hadn't intended to, she only wanted to take a little, but she kept on sucking. It was magical, better than anything she had ever tasted or felt. Stopping seemed impossible, but she knew she must. She would not kill this girl.

Ava suddenly threw her onto the snow and ran. She leaned against a building, and wondered why she wasn't gasping for breath. Her breathing had become so shallow – just like Nathan's when he'd tried to kill her.

The shard of mirror was still in her hand, smeared with blood. Ava looked back, but the girl was gone. The end of a black coat disappeared around a corner. A chill ran through Ava: someone *was* following her after all.

five

Ava stumbled into her hotel bathroom. She felt sick with self-loathing but couldn't vomit.

Maybe vampires can't be sick, she thought.

Her head was reeling – partly with the excitement of the blood and partly with horror at what she'd done, what she'd become. How could she live like this? But she needed the blood. She just knew it. It was as necessary as breathing.

It was horrible, but she hadn't killed anyone. She'd hold back; she wouldn't kill. Then they wouldn't become vampires. That was how it worked, wasn't it?

It was rationalising, she knew. Ava had to excuse what she was doing, because she couldn't stop doing it. She stood in the shower for a long time, trying to wash away the taint of wanting blood. There was no blood on her, not a drop – but she felt filthy.

The next morning, she slept late. She wished, now, that she'd stayed longer in Ignace's castle and found out about life as a vampire. But he'd sent her away. He'd said they'd be watching her, and if she told anyone ... She shivered.

Were they watching her? Maybe they'd help

her. *Because I really can't do this alone*, she thought. She wondered if the tall man who'd stared at her was working for Ignace. She hoped not. For no reason she could explain, he'd frightened her.

Ava turned on the TV, hoping for distraction, but there was nothing in English. The local station showed pictures of the police cordon near the circus, and then of the place where Ava had attacked the woman. She couldn't understand the commentary. Grainy photos of both women came on screen, with a number to contact underneath.

Ava felt sick. Someone, somewhere, had made a connection between the attacks already.

She walked out into the street, desperate to get away. People went about their daily lives, going to work, shopping, trooping through the snow and the slush. They didn't stare at her. She didn't look like a vampire, then. She didn't look like a monster people should avoid.

She could smell them, though. They smelled enticing. Even a tramp slumped in a doorway had a smell that drew her towards him. It was a smell she had never noticed about people before, a slightly muffled smell. But the smell of blood, all the same.

She stopped at the café and had another rare steak. That calmed her interest in the people. As she ate, she saw a tall dark figure through the mist on the window, looking in at her. That man, again – was it? She couldn't be sure, but her skin prickled at the thought. When she left the café, there was no one there. She hurried, head down, listening hard for footsteps behind her.

She set off for the park where the circus was pitched. She felt dirty, and she was afraid to face Ivan. But *he* would understand, if he were a vampire. And she was drawn to him. He was cute, and funny, as well as perhaps a vampire.

It was dusk as Ava picked her way between the trailers and tents. The police were gone, the tape taken down, but a bunch of flowers lay wilting on the ground near the tiger trailer. Her stomach lurched. Flowers? Why? She had only bitten the woman.

She found Ivan's trailer – it was easy enough as it said '*Vampir*' in large red letters and had a picture of a caped vampire dripping blood.

'Ivan?' she called as she knocked. 'Are you in your coffin or can I come in?'

He opened the door immediately. He was dressed in jeans and a shabby jumper, and it was only when he spoke and she saw his filed and built-up teeth that there was anything of the vampire about him. It looked odd, the jumper and those teeth. But the magic was still there: something unspeakably enticing about him.

'Lovely to see you!' he cried, waving his arms around. 'I didn't expect you'd ever come – but this is great.'

He swept her into the smoky warmth of the trailer. There was no coffin, but a narrow bed used as a sofa. The smoke and the warmth came from a wood-burning stove. Ivan swept a pile of comics from a small wooden table onto the sofa and pulled up a stool.

'Sit? Would you like something? Tea? Something stronger?'

'Let's start with tea.' Ava smiled. She let the warmth and the oddness of Ivan's caravan fold around her and she relaxed into talking to this strange, strange boy. She didn't know or care where this evening would go – but she was up for the ride.

Six

They talked for hours. Ava felt secure, buffered against the horrors inside her head. She was drunk on Ivan, light-headed with having fun again. Perhaps, even, falling in love slightly, she thought. Did she trust herself to fall in love again after Nathan? Ivan was different, though – and she was different.

It was dark when she made her way back from the park. Snow swirled so thickly in large, cartoon flakes that it was hard to see. She didn't expect there to be anyone out tonight. But there was a skinny, stooped man leaning in a doorway coughing. He must have been fifty at least. His skin was tired and grey from smoking, and his eyes were blank. He stepped out of the doorway to ask Ava for money.

Ava reached into her pocket for coins, and her fingers found the piece of mirror. The reality of what she was came crashing back to her. At the same moment, she saw a scratch on the man's bare arm – a line of dull, drying, dark red blood. The longing came over her so quickly she couldn't stop herself. Ava grabbed his hand and pulled it to her mouth, then sank her teeth into it.

The man screamed and screamed, thrashing at Ava's head and shoulders with his other arm, but she didn't let go. She sucked and swallowed and felt the warmth flood through her again. At last she tore herself away and ran off, leaving the man yowling.

As she passed a side street, Ava saw the same tall figure she'd seen before. He was wrapped in a long coat. He had a hat pulled down over his brow and a scarf over his mouth, but his eyes gleamed brightly between them as though he were smiling.

The warmth the blood had spread through her body was gone in an instant – those cold, knowing eyes chilled her to the core. Ava wanted to run, but didn't dare in case he ran after her. There was something about him, something odd that she couldn't pin down and that made her feel instantly sick with fear. It was a feeling both of evil and of some strange familiarity – as though she knew him and knew he was very bad.

Panicked, Ava ran; she was almost as terrified that he'd seen what she'd done as that he'd catch her. But when she turned and glanced over her shoulder, the man was hurrying the way she'd come, towards the screaming man. She was relieved, but alarmed – was he going to help? What would he think of Ava, running in the other direction? She didn't care, as long as he didn't come near her.

Back at the hotel, she showered and tried to calm her nerves. The man hadn't followed her to the hotel – she prayed he didn't know where she was staying. Somewhere in the night she heard the wail of a siren. Police or ambulance? It had taken a long time, if it were for the man she'd attacked.

She shuddered, thinking of him taken away to hospital, telling them what had happened, seeing the disbelief or horror on the doctors' faces. Would they believe him? What if they spoke to her stalker? Had he seen her do it? It wouldn't take long to put the three cases together and realise he was telling the truth – especially now the first two had been on television.

Seven

'Truth or dare?'

Ivan slammed down a tiny, chipped beaker in front of Ava. Thick red liquid slopped up the inside.

She was back in his trailer, unable to keep away. The rickety table rocked and the lamp flickered. Ava laughed and hooked a strand of hair behind her ear. She felt safe here, with Ivan. She could put the horror and guilt of last night out of her mind.

'Truth,' she said.

'Do you have a boyfriend?'

'Not any more,' Ava said.

'What happened?'

'Not fair – that's a second question.' Ava looked down, twisted her fingers together. Nathan's face floated into her mind and she shook her head to get rid of it. 'My turn. Truth or dare?'

'Truth.'

'Are you really a vampire?'

Ivan downed the drink and sloshed more into the glass from a jug.

'Trade secret. Now you – truth or dare?'

'Dare.'

'Bite me. Let's see if you could do my trade.'

'I can't. I'll do anything else – but not bite.'

'No – only biting will do. Drink, then.'

Ava knocked back the drink.

'It's blood,' she gasped. Her whole body thrilled to it. It took all her will power not to grab the jug and down it all.

Ivan laughed. 'Of course. But you did it!'

Ava refilled the glass. She closed her eyes in pleasure and Ivan raised an eyebrow.

'Strange girl,' he said. 'Dare.'

Ava's mind was full of the blood. She couldn't

think of anything – least of all a dare.

'Handstand.'

'What? That's tame! What's got into you?'

'I can't think of anything I want you to do.'

'What, not anything?' He stroked her face, then leaned in to kiss her. He tasted good. Ava put a hand on the back of his head and drew him towards her as soon as he started to pull away.

'Wow. Have we finished this game?' he said at last.

'Nope. You haven't done the handstand.'

Ivan stood up, bowed, then did a handstand on one hand. He held it for thirty seconds, jumped upright, and bowed again. Ava clapped.

'I live in a circus, remember,' he said. 'It's as if I

dared you to breathe. One more round. You – truth or dare?' Ava hoped he wouldn't dare her to breathe.

'Truth.'

Ivan slammed the drink down in front of her.

'Why won't you bite me?'

'Because I'm a vampire,' she said.

'No way? Me too. So that's OK, you can bite me.'

'No, seriously. You wouldn't answer my question. You wouldn't say if you really are. And I am,' Ava said.

'Prove it. Bite me.'

'No.'

'I want you to,' he said.

'I know. But that's not enough.'

He leaned over and kissed her again.

'What if I bit you?' he whispered.

They kissed, long and hungrily. He hooked her long blonde hair behind her ear to bare her neck and traced his tongue along a blue vein. Then he pushed the sweater from her shoulder. The skin glowed pale gold and smooth in the dim light of the lamp.

Ivan kissed her shoulder, played his tongue over it until he found the warm, plump top of her arm and then, ever so slowly at first, sank his pointed fangs into the flesh. Ava gasped with excitement and alarm, and Ivan sucked long and hard. When he raised his head she looked into his eyes, expecting to see passion. But she saw only fear.

She looked down at her shoulder. Two holes marked the place he had bitten. Two slightly pinkish holes. They both looked at the holes and waited. It seemed hours before Ivan spoke.

'You don't bleed.'

'No. Well, I do eventually. But slowly. I told you, I'm a vampire,' Ava replied.

'There's no such thing as vampires.'

'What?' Ava stared at him, her eyes wide with horror, matching his. 'But – you're a vampire. Aren't you? You drink blood, you have the teeth, you ... '

'Think. Where are you?' he cried. 'This is a circus for heaven's sake! I'm a circus act!'

Ava pointed to the jug of blood.

'Where's that from?'

'Butcher. It's animal blood. You didn't really

think it was human, did you? Did you?'

Ava was afraid to say that it didn't taste human, but she'd assumed that was because it wasn't fresh. Ivan was backing away now.

'You – was it you? The lugat?'

'Lugat? What's that?' She remembered the word the woman near the tiger cage had shouted that first night at the circus.

'It's an Albanian word for vampire. The lugat bites, but rarely kills. It weakens its victims, and sometimes makes them lust for blood, too. It doesn't have pointy teeth, like this' – he bared his dramatic fangs – 'but has ordinary teeth, like you. And makes an ordinary, ugly bite. Like the bite on Donka.'

'Who?'

'One of our performers.'

Dread gripped Ava's stomach. The circus woman – she was a person, with a name, with friends. And one of her friends was Ivan. He carried on:

'She was bitten by someone near the tiger cage. Someone who didn't bleed when ripped up by the – ' He stopped. He looked at her bandaged arm. 'Take the bandage off.'

'Is that a dare?' Ava wanted to make light of it, get back to where they were before. She didn't want to spoil this, didn't want to lose him.

'No. It's an order.'

Ava ignored the order.

'Where is she? Is she OK?' she asked.

'What? No, of course not. She's dead. Like the others.'

'Others? You said lugats don't kill people.'

'They don't usually. Or so the Albanians say. But it looks like they're wrong in your case. You did it, didn't you? You killed those people. You're a psycho – a sick psycho!' Ivan had now backed away to the kitchen of his trailer and was feeling around behind him for a knife.

'No!' Ava cried. 'No! I've never killed anyone! I swear I haven't!'

'You expect me to believe that? Even I've been blamed for it and I'm not a real vampire! Three people have been found dead – well, Donka was found dying – bitten and knifed, and you expect me to believe it's not you? That by some amazing coincidence, a real vampire turns up here at the same time as a different psycho-killer who happens to bite people? Come on!'

'Ivan –'

'I'm not called Ivan! It's an act! My name's Darren and I am NOT a vampire. You, though – who are you? Where are you from? Are you dead?'

He had found the knife now – a long bread knife. He held it out in front of him. Ava saw the fear in his face and his hand trembling.

'You can't hurt me with that. Not enough. You know that! If anyone knows it, you do.'

'Did you kill them?' His voice was high and quivery.

'NO! NO, I DIDN'T,' she shouted. 'I bit some people, yes. But I've never killed anyone. I don't

have a clue what you're talking about. I don't even
have a knife,' she added. 'But you do.'

'You think *I* did it?' he stuttered.

'No. I didn't even know it had happened.'

They stood looking at each other.

'I'm sorry,' he said at last. 'But you can see how
it looks. It's a surprise, a real vampire in my
caravan.' He gave a nervous laugh.

'Please put the knife down,' she said.

'I won't hurt you – there's no point, as you said.'

'No. But I might hurt you if you cut yourself.'

She walked over to him, took the knife from his
hand, and kissed him gently on the lips.

Eight

It was very late when Ava left Ivan's trailer. Or Darren's – but she preferred to think of him as Ivan. As she stepped out of the door, someone moved in the shadow of the trees. A man in a long coat and a hat, waiting. Waiting for her.

She gripped Ivan's hand too tightly and pointed to the trees. A glint of steel in the moonlight, and the man was gone.

'I'm afraid,' Ava said. Ivan took her in his arms.

'Do you want to stay? Go home in daylight?'

She nodded. 'But – '

'I know.'

'No, I mean the man. I've seen him before. He's been following me.'

Ivan drew her back into the trailer and locked the door.

'Are you sure? For how long?'

'I don't know exactly. A few days. And he saw me ... '

' ... Bite someone?'

'Yes.' She looked down, ashamed. Ivan was no

longer her refuge from the horror. She had to face up to it even here.

'And these people were alive when you left them? You swear?'

'I swear,' Ava said.

'I don't think he'll harm you,' Ivan said. 'I think he's a vulture. He wants those people; not you.'

'You mean – he killed them?'

'That would be my guess.'

'Why?'

'I have no idea. Why do psychos ever kill people? Because they're psychos. Come here,' he said. 'He won't harm you, but you can stay.' He folded her into his arms.

'But I haven't hurt anyone tonight.'

'He didn't know what would happen when you came here. The first time you came here, there was Donka. Perhaps he hoped ... ' Ivan's voice trailed off.

Ava shuddered.

'I don't want to be alone. Not ever.' She snuggled into Ivan's jumper and his arms. At that moment, they both heard it: the tread of a boot in snow. Then a scratching noise by the door.

'He's on the steps to the trailer,' Ivan whispered.

'There's no one there,' Ava whispered back. Ivan looked at her.

'But you can hear him.'

'We can hear something. But no one is there. I can smell – people. Blood. Always. I can smell your blood. I can smell the blood we drank earlier. I can't smell him. I can't smell anyone at the door.'

'Dare,' said Ivan. 'Open the door.'

Ava was certain. She couldn't smell blood – he couldn't be there. But as she approached the door that certainty wavered. She did hear a noise. But even if it were an animal she would smell its blood. The whole world smelled of blood to her now. She turned the key, and paused. Ivan stood behind her, his arms around her waist.

'Well?' he said. 'Still sure?'

She opened the door.

And there he was.

The long coat was white with snow, a cracked cake of it over the shoulders. The dim light from the trailer fell on his face, making a pattern of deep shadows in which she could make out only his eyes, a twisting half-smile and a neat beard. A handsome face, she thought, but not attractive. A long blade glinted in one hand.

'Well,' he said. 'This is a surprise, isn't it? Hello, little vampire.'

Nine

Ava took a step back, but didn't close the door.

'Who are you? You don't ... '

'I don't smell?' he said. 'Well, I should hope not. I had a shower. Nor do you.' But the man did not smile. Nor did he raise his knife. He looked past her into the room, to the jug on the table and the two shot glasses.

'Aren't you going to offer me a drink?' he asked.

'I don't think you'd like it,' Ava answered.

'Oh, I think you're wrong there,' he said. 'May I?'

His eyes gleamed with a desire that Ava was afraid to deny.

'Pour him a drink, Ivan,' she said. 'Please. Do it.'

Ivan slipped from behind her and poured a double shot. The man downed it licked around his lips and his teeth. His pointy teeth.

'You're –' Ava started.

'Well spotted,' he said. 'Yes. One of your kind. I'm surprised you didn't notice that he' – he raised his knife to point at Ivan – 'is not. He smells.'

'And vampires don't? I didn't know,' Ava said.

'How are you liking it, little vampire?'

She said nothing. She wasn't liking it one bit.

'You're not good. You leave a mess. Someone has to tidy it up. Tut tut.' He waved his knife. 'You can't just leave them lying around, you know. They – turn. And we don't want too many.'

'Turn?'

'Haven't you read any vampire books? Seen any vampire films? *Dracula*? *Twilight*? *Buffy*? *Cirque du Freak*?' He looked at Ivan. 'Hasn't your little wannabe-vampire told you anything?'

'You mean,' said Ava, 'those people would become vampires?'

'They could have done. But luckily for you, I was here to clear up the mess.'

'You killed them?' Ava didn't want to hear the answer. But she already knew.

'Don't thank me. It was my pleasure.' He bowed. 'It makes a nice change from rare steaks and stray dogs.'

'What are you doing here? Why are you following me?' Ava asked at last.

The man pointed at Ivan with his knife. 'I thought he might be your next snack. And someone has to clear up after you. Grazing – it's not the done thing. Finish them off and make sure they don't come back. I'm surprised Ignace didn't tell you all that.'

'Ignace?' Ava said. 'You know him?'

The man almost laughed, but it was more a shout of 'Hah!'

'Everyone knows Ignace. Even those outside his

cosy group. Rogue vampires, as he calls us. He didn't even tell you we existed, did he?'

Ava shook her head.

'Ignace doesn't know I'm a vampire,' she said. 'He thought I was immune.'

The man was suddenly interested.

'Doesn't, he now? Well, well.

'Ignace is a fool,' he said. 'His huge vampire research centre hasn't discovered what I've found out on my own – no one is immune. Sometimes it's quick, and sometimes it's slow. But they all turn. You have to kill them. Thoroughly. Every time.'

'Who are you?' Ava asked at last.

'You want my name? Guess. And it's not

Rumpelstiltskin.'

'I can't,' Ava said.

'No. No one ever has. You like games, don't you? You've been playing a game here, I see. Give me another drink.'

Ivan poured another shot and the man swallowed it, closed his eyes in pleasure, and sighed.

'Time for a game. Let's play my favourite. Hangman. Aren't you going to invite me in?'

'NO!' shouted Ivan. 'A vampire can't cross the threshold unless invited. And then he can come in whenever he wants. You're NOT invited!'

The man gave his odd shout of laughter again.

'Is it true?' Ava asked him. He shrugged.

'I've no idea. But it would be very rude of me to come in if you didn't invite me. Bring the table. We can play right here in the doorway.'

Neither Ava nor Ivan moved.

'I want to play a game and I'm the one with the sharpest knife. Bring the table.'

Ivan bristled. He didn't want to take orders from a stranger in his own trailer.

'Go on,' whispered Ava. *He's dangerous,* she thought, willing Ivan to read her mind.

Ten

Ivan dragged the table to the door, making the jug wobble. The man removed one of his leather gloves, dipped a finger in the jug and sucked it hungrily. He dipped again and drew on the table in blood:

_ _ _ _ / _ _ _ / _ _ _ _ _ _

'You can work together,' he said. 'It's the name I'm known by, not my real name. You will have heard it, I'm sure.'

'E,' said Ivan. The stranger dipped his finger in the blood.

_ _ _ _ / _ _ E / _ _ _ _ E _

'A'

_ A _ _ / _ _ E / _ _ _ _ E _

'I'

_ A _ _ / _ _ E / _ I _ _ E _

'O.'

The man drew a line in blood. 'Do you have some wood? I prefer to build a real scaffold. There's no point playing hangman if no one gets hanged.'

'U?' Ivan said.

The stranger drew another line at right angles to the first.

'T,' said Ava.

_ A _ _ / T _ E / _ I _ _ E _

'S,' Ivan said.

The stranger drew the top bar of a scaffold.

'We can use a tree if you don't have any wood,'
he said.

Ivan was visibly shaking, but Ava put a hand on
his arm.

'Don't worry,' she whispered. 'We're going to win.
You just have to think. Which names are T space E?'

'Tee, Tie, Toe, The. Nothing else,' Ivan said.

'H,' Ava said.

The man dipped his finger in the blood, then

filled in the H.

_ A _ _ / T H E / _ I _ _ E _

'N,' Ivan guessed.

The stranger drew a crossbar to support the scaffold. 'You'll need a rope, too,' he said. 'Or a scarf. It would be a shame if a nice young boy like you hanged himself because he fell for a female serial killer, wouldn't it?' He grinned, his pointy teeth resting on his lower lip.

'R,' said Ava.

The stranger sniffed, dipped his finger, and added two Rs. 'Getting warmer,' he said.

_ A _ _ / T H E / R I _ _ E R

'What words can we make that fit R-I-space-

space-E-R?' asked Ivan.

Ava went white as it dawned on her. She didn't want Ivan to see it, but how could he not?

'I think we've had enough of this game,' she said, looking the stranger in the eyes. Now he laughed properly.

'Good girl,' he said. 'Do you want to share with vampire boy?'

Ivan looked from one to the other.

'Who is he?' he asked Ava.

The man held out a hand.

'Jack,' he said. 'And you are?'

'Jack who?'

Eleven

The man dipped his finger in the jug and filled in the rest of the letters.

JACK/THE/RIPPER

'Slow, vampire boy, very slow.' He completed the stick scaffold and drew a hanged man on it. Before Ivan could blink, Jack reached across the table and grabbed him by the neck, squeezing hard.

'You'd be hanged if you didn't have the clever

girlfriend. Hanged and worse. Count yourself lucky. This time.' He let go, and Ivan choked and gasped for breath.

'So – aren't you going to bite him? I didn't come only to play games, you know.'

'No,' Ava said. 'I'm not going to bite him. And he's mine – so keep off.'

Jack shrugged. 'I will do absolutely whatever I wish to do,' he said. 'Do you think I am afraid of anyone?'

'Ignace –'

'Hah! Ignace? Two-bit dictator who fancies himself king of the world! And he doesn't even know you're here – you said so yourself. You're with me now. And if you're not with me ... ' he drew a finger across his throat. 'I'm pretty good at that, as you may recall. Whitechapel, London, 1888. The legend lives on. Plenty since, but I stopped showing off. It makes life – tricky.'

'Are you going to kill me?' Ava asked.

'Good grief, no. You're more fun alive. A beginner – fresh blood. I love it. And this –' he pointed at Ivan again – 'you want to keep it for a while? Fair enough. Just tell me when you're sick of it and I'll help with the necessary.' He showed his teeth and leered at Ivan. 'Or we could share it now ...'

'No!' Ava grabbed a handful of Ivan's jumper and pulled him closer to her.

'Well, now I've introduced myself I'll leave you in peace for the evening. I'm happy to go on tidying up for you. But you'll attract Ignace's attention. He has his spies, you know, even here.

Let's keep out of his way, shall we?'

'There is no 'we'!' Ava said.

Jack smiled – a nasty, sly, confident smile.

'I think you'll find you're mistaken, little vampire. You don't have the ProVamp Ignace hands out to his vampires to control their hunger for blood. And you've already found that it doesn't take many bitings to attract attention. They're onto you, you know – not Ignace, the police.'

'But I didn't kill them!' Ava shouted. 'You did!'

'*They* don't know that. Someone remarkably like you was seen nearby ... I'm good at slipping away unseen. Lots of practice, you see.

'You need me. I'll look after you, little vampire. Just like Ignace gives his vampires a mentor, a guardian – I'll be yours. Juliette has Ignace, Finn has mad Lorenzo – you have Jack the Ripper!'

Ava gripped Ivan's jumper. She felt sick, faint – how could this happen?

'What's your real name?' Ivan asked suddenly. 'When you're not Jack?'

'Do you want to play again?' Jack asked.

'No. Just tell me. Please.'

'Why should I?'

'Because I know every way of harming a vampire and I want to know,' Ivan said. Ava gripped his arm. His bravery frightened her.

Jack paused. 'Origen Hobbs,' he said at last.

'Not one of the usual suspects?' Ivan said.

'Not a suspect at all. You'll find no trace. I'm good. Very good. I'll be seeing you – both. Later.'

Ava buried her face in Ivan's chest as Jack the Ripper walked down the snowy steps and into the darkness, the knife glinting in his hand.

'Well,' Ava said as the snow blew into the caravan, 'we're going to have to find Ignace. Somehow.'

'We?'

'Yes.' She took Ivan's hand. 'We. There is a 'we', isn't there?'

He nodded, and leaned over to kiss her. Snowflakes caught in her eyelashes, and he brushed them away gently.

'Yes. We will find Ignace. Whoever he is.'

Vampire Dawn

The story starts with **Die Now or Live Forever**. Read it first.

Then follow each individual's story. You can read these in any order:

Juliette's story

Finn's story

Omar's story

Alistair and Ruby's story

Ava's story

Plus an essential guide for new vampires.

Find out more at www.vampiredawn.co.uk. Follow the vampires on Facebook: www.facebook.com/VampireDawnBooks

twitter: @vampiredawn